THE LOST DINOSAUR

Story By
Bill Graham

Illustrations By
Genevieve Meek

Software By
Sally Graham

COPYRIGHT © 1989 by *About Me!* Personalized Children's Books

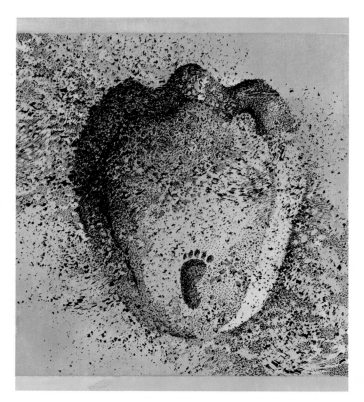

This Book is About Me!
Lyndsey B. Paparella

Happy 8th Birthday!
With Love From
Auntie Joan, Uncle Ray and Stefanie
1990

It was a sunny afternoon in Warwick.
Lyndsey Paparella, age eight, felt like going
somewhere. "Let's go to the museum today
to see the dinosaurs," said Lyndsey. David,
Stefanie and Eric thought that was a great
idea. Soon they were off.

The museum was having a special dinosaur
exhibit. There were skeletons and footprints of
real dinosaurs. There were man-made dinosaurs
that moved and looked like the real thing.

Lyndsey was amazed at how alive the
dinosaurs looked. The tour guide pointed to
one and asked, "Does anyone know the name
of this dinosaur?" Lyndsey raised her hand
and said, "That is easy. It's a
Tyrannosaurus." "You really know your
dinosaurs," said the guide.

"The Tyrannosaurus walked on its hind legs. It was a ferocious monster," the tour guide went on. When the children looked at its sharp teeth, no one doubted what he said.

"This is a Triceratops. Notice the three horns on its head." Everyone loved to see the different kinds of dinosaurs, but all the ones they had seen so far were really scary.

While the others were looking at Triceratops, Lyndsey saw something strange going on behind her. It was a cute baby Brachiosaurus looking right at Lyndsey. "Come here," it seemed to say. Was it real or was it one of the man-made dinosaurs?

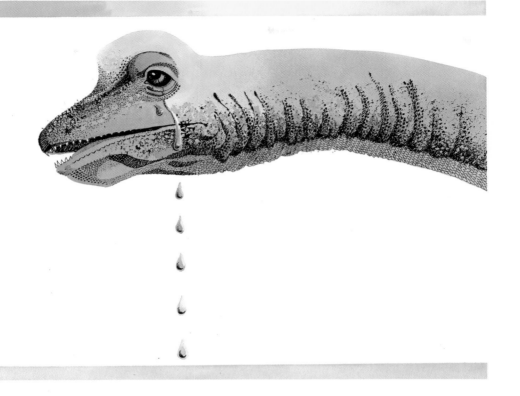

"Lyndsey, I need your help," said the little dinosaur. "My name is Brenu. I'm a baby Brachiosaurus and I am lost." Tears were in his eyes. "You are real!" said Lyndsey. "I thought you were a machine. How did you get here?"

Then Brenu told his story. "I am not supposed to be here. Yesterday I was eating tree leaves with my mother and my sisters. When I awoke today I was in this strange place with these machines that look like dinosaurs. I know my mother is worried. Where am I?" cried Brenu.

"You must be in a time warp," said Lyndsey. "It seems impossible, but you are here in Warwick in 1990. There are no dinosaurs in my time. You are in a museum. Somehow you came from 150 million years ago. I will try to help you go back home."

This would not be easy. Was time travel even possible? There are many stories about going back in time, but could it really be done? Brenu the Brachiosaurus got here somehow. There must be a way to send the poor creature back.

The tour guide said, "Thank you all for taking the dinosaur tour. You are now invited to enjoy the rest of the museum. There are many wonderful things to see here."

"I've got it!" thought Lyndsey. "It just might work." She was standing in front of a very old time machine. It was built by an inventor over 100 years ago. Nobody thought it could actually do anything, let alone go back in time. Lyndsey ran back to the dinosaur exhibit.

"Come with me," Lyndsey whispered. "I have found a time machine." "A what?" asked Brenu. "There's no time to explain," said Lyndsey. "We have to sneak over to it. Hurry." When they got to the machine Brenu got in while Lyndsey set the dials.

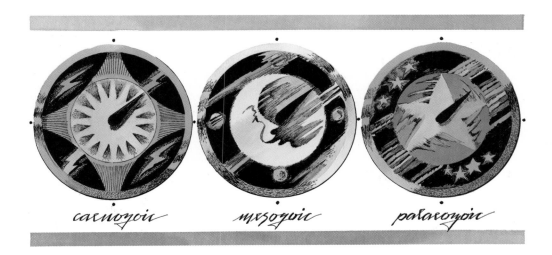

cenozoic   mesozoic   palaeozoic

The time machine looked funny with a baby dinosaur sitting in it. Thank goodness no one was looking. At first nothing happened. "At least we tried," said a sad Brenu. Suddenly the machine came to life. Lights flashed. Bells rang. It shook once, then began to fade away.

"Goodbye, Lyndsey. Thank you so much..."
said Brenu, as he vanished from sight.
David, Stefanie and Eric walked up just after
the time machine disappeared. "Are you
ready to go, Lyndsey?"

"Yes, I am ready. I was just coming to find you so we could go home." Brenu, the baby Brachiosaurus, was already home.

ABOUT ME !

Personalized Children's Books
Order Form

For information call: L & M Creations 401-647-2335

( ) Indicate Selection:

( ) **The Circus Star** *
( ) **The Lost Dinosaur**
( ) **The Balloon Ride**
( ) **If I Could Be...**
( ) **Imagine That!**
( ) **A Birthday Mystery**
( ) **My First Book**
( ) **Santa's Secret Helper**
( ) **The Hanukkah Rescue**
( ) **My ABC's Crayon Book**
( ) **Personalized Santa Letter**
( ) **My First Book Gift Certificate**
( ) **Photosticker**

* Also Available in ( ) Spanish and ( ) French.
Indicate with (x) language desired.

Giftgiver's Information:
(please print clearly)

Name:

Street:

City:

State: Zip:

Phone No. of person ordering book:

Giftgiver's name as it will appear in book

(ex. Mom and Dad, Aunt Betty, etc)

Enter Childs Information:
(please print clearly)

First name: M.I.:

Last Name:

Street:

City:

State: Zip:

Boy: ( )   Girl ( )

Age:

Nickname:

Birthdate:

Birthplace:

(optional, for my first book only)

List Three Friends/Relatives Names:

1.

2.

3.

Mail Book, Certificate or Letter to:

Name:

Street

City:

State: Zip:

Ordering Information:

	each	total
About Me! Book	$9.95	
My 1st Bk. Gift Cert	$11.45	
ABC Crayon Book	$4.95	
Santa Letter	$2.49	
Photosticker	$0.89	
Shipping (per book)	$1.50	
Subtotal		
R.I. Residents add 7% sales tax		
Total		

Mail Your Order To:

L & M Creations

81 Carpenter Road
Foster, R.I. 02825
401-647-2335